A New Fable of the Grasshopper and the Ant

JOHN J. PLENTY
and FIDDLER DAN

By JOHN CIARDI

ILLUSTRATIONS BY MADELEINE GEKIERE

J. B. Lippincott Company. Philadelphia and New York

This book is for
PETER CARNEY
Benn's good friend and my good friend,
because he is all boy and a noise wide,
and because he and Benn together make
one of the happiest noises my house shakes to.

Ten years ago, or maybe twenty,
There lived an ant named John J. Plenty.
And every day, come rain, come shine,
John J. would take his place in line
With all the other ants. All day
He hunted seeds to haul away,
Or beetle eggs, or bits of bread.

These he would carry on his head
Back to his house. And John J., he
Was happy as an ant can be
When he was carrying a load
Big as a barn along the road.

The work was hard, but all John J.—
Or any other ant—would say
Was "More! Get more! No time to play!
Winter is coming!"

So all day,
All summer long, while birds were singing,
John J. Plenty kept on bringing
Beetle eggs, and crumbs, and seeds,

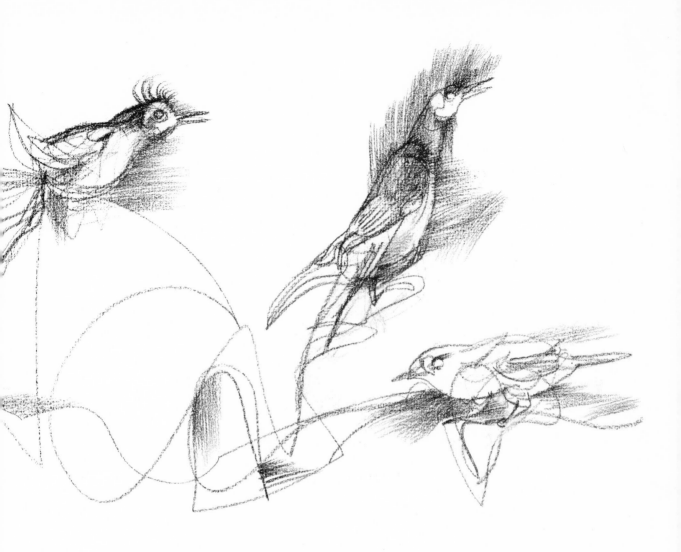

Moth-hams, flower-fuzz, salad-weeds,

Grub-sausages, the choicer cuts

Of smoked bees, aphid butter, nuts,

And everything else you ever thought of

That ants prefer to have a lot of.

As soon as he put one load away
In his cellar bin, he would turn and say,
"More! Get more! No time to play!
Winter is coming!"

                    Now, sad to tell,
John J. had a sister and loved her well,
Until one day she met—alas!—
A grasshopper hopping about in the grass
And playing the fiddle, and wrong or right,
(Though it's rare among ants)

                              it was love at first sight.

"Don't!" cried John J. "You'll come a cropper!"
But he couldn't stop long enough to stop her,
For winter was coming, as you recall,
And there was a load he just *had* to haul.

So John J. Plenty's sister ran

Away with the grasshopper. Fiddler Dan,

His name was. All *he* ever carried

Was the fiddle he fiddled. Well, they married.

And all day long from rose to rose

Dan played the music the summer knows,

Of the sun and rain through the tall corn rows,

And of time as it comes, and of love as it grows.

And all the summer stirred to hear

The voice of the music. Far and near

The grasses swayed, and the sun and shade

Danced to the love the music played.

And Dan played on for the world to turn,

While his little wife lay on a fringe of fern,

And heard the heart of summer ringing,
Sad and sweet to the fiddle's singing.

So the sun came up and the sun went down.
So summer changed from green to brown.

So autumn changed from brown to gold.

And the music sang, "The world grows old,

But never my song. The song stays new,

My sad sweet love, as the thought of you."

And summer and autumn dreamed and found

The name of the world in that sad sweet sound

Of the music telling how time grows old.

Fields held their breath to hear it told.

The trees bent down from the hills to hear.

A flower uncurled to shed a tear

For the sound of the music. And field and hill

Woke from that music, sad and still.

John J. Plenty trudged along

With a load and a half. He heard the song.

He heard the music far and near.

"Get more!" he cried. "It's almost here!

Winter is coming! As for those two—

Let them fiddle on. I have work to do!

Let them fiddle the hairs right off the bow.

When once it comes time for the ice and snow,

You can bet that fiddle of theirs will fall still.

They had better stay away from my hill

When that time comes." So said John J.,

As he carried his load and a half away.

"They'll get nothing from me!" So said John J.

And sure enough, there came a day

When the snow came down. It came to stay.

It chilled from forty to thirty to twenty.

"Just as I said," said John J. Plenty.

It chilled from twenty to ten to zero.

"I must shut the door," said our provident hero.

He knew the music had fallen still.

But just to be sure, he stood on the sill

And listened and listened—not a sound.

Not a song to be heard for miles around.

"Just as I told them!" John J. said.

And he shut his door.

And he went to bed.

He woke up hungry. He looked at his food
Piled high as the ceiling, and all of it good.

"Well, now, some moth-ham would be fine.
With two poached beetle-eggs—divine!
And maybe a glass of thistle-wine!"
And so John J. sat down to dine.

He had, in fact, heaped up his plate,

When a voice inside him cried out—"Wait!

What if *this* time the winter stayed on

Until all your hard-earned food was gone?

You had better wait a day or two

To see what winter is going to do.

You worked so hard to carry this stuff,

But can you be sure you carried *enough?*"

So John J. Plenty waited and fasted.

As for the winter, it lasted . . .

. . . and lasted.

He nibbled a crumb one day in ten.
But he shook with terror even then
When he thought of how he might be wasting
All that food he was hardly tasting.
And that's how it went.

Until at last

The sun grew warm and the winter passed.
Then John J. Plenty stirred once more,
Sighed with relief, admired his store
Of untouched food, and thought:

"GET MORE!

I've learned my lesson. This year I
Will stack my food up twice as high!
Then let winter stay and stay—
I'll eat all night, I'll eat all day!

I've learned my lesson. More! Get more!"
He said.

                And started out the door.
He hadn't found his first good load.
In fact, he hadn't reached the road,
When he stopped and listened.

                        And what did he hear,
But the music sounding far and near!
From far and near, from blade to blade,
He heard the song the springtime played.
It's a softer fiddle than autumn knows
When the fiddler goes down tall corn rows,
But the same far song. It grows and grows,
And spring and summer stir to hear
The music sounding far and near.

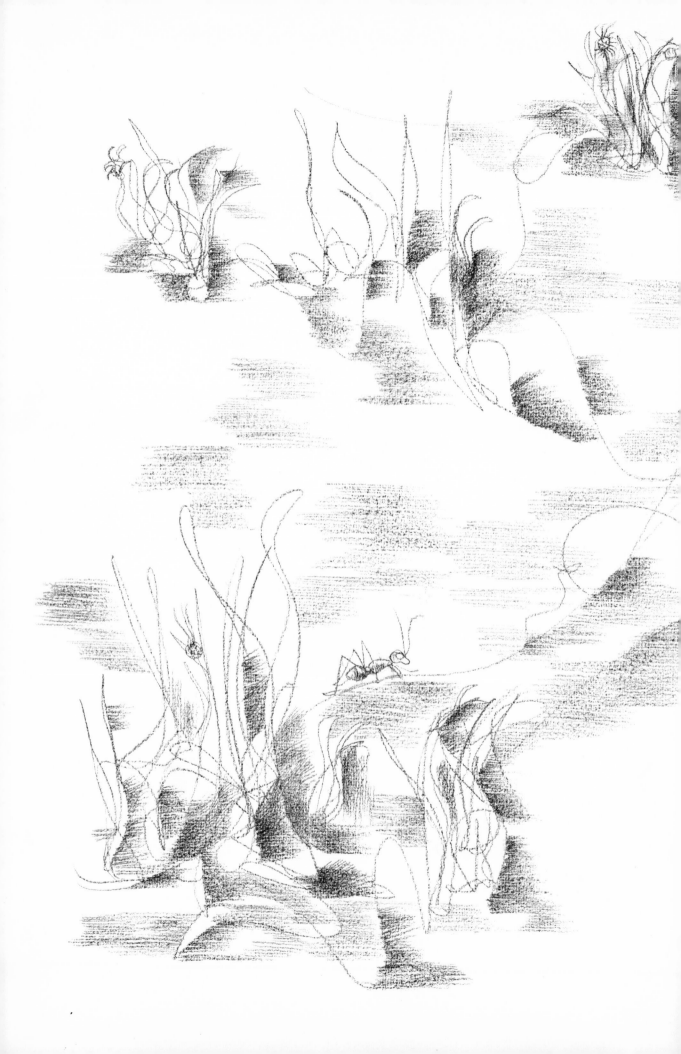

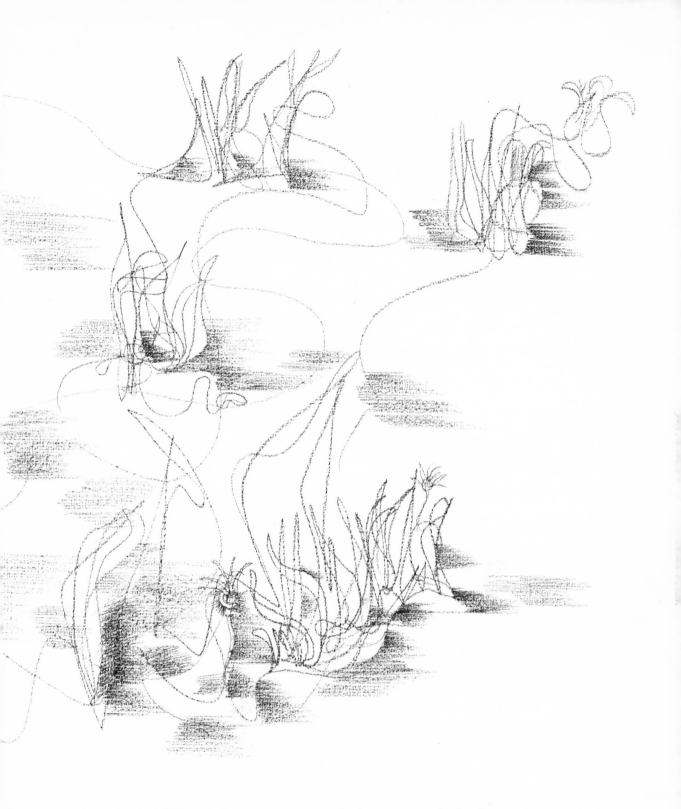

And the grasses sway, and the sun and shade
Dance when they hear the music played.

It was Dan, still singing for time to turn
While his little wife lay on a fringe of fern
And heard the heart of the springtime ringing
Sweet and new as the fiddle's singing.

John J. Plenty—ah, my dears!—
Listened, and couldn't believe his ears!
Or maybe he was too weak on his feet
From all that food he hadn't dared eat.
He took one wobbly step, and—*flop!*
He fell on his face and had to stop.

He fell on his face and he couldn't move.
While the music sang its sad sweet love.

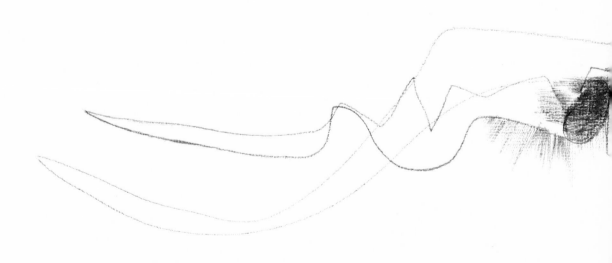

And he had to listen all night and all day
To what the music had to say.

He had to listen all day and all night
While the music sang the birds to flight,
The flowers to bloom, the trees to bud.

And there lay John J.—in the mud!

I guess he recovered. I hope he did.

I don't know where the Fiddler hid

With his pretty wife from the ice and snow.

I guess about all I really know

Is—*save a little or save a lot,*

You have to eat some of what you've got.

And—*say what you like as you trudge along,*

The world won't turn without a song.

And—*Fiddlers grow thin and their hands turn blue*
When winter comes, but they pull through.
There's this about music—and, oh, it's true!—
It never stays stopped.   Just listen, and you
Will hear it start over, as sweet and new
As the first pale leaves and the first spring dew.

—And that's what John J. never knew.